This book belongs to:

_____

I celebrated World Book Day 2019 with
this gift from my local bookseller,
Sibéal Pounder, Jason Cockcroft,
Laura Ellen Anderson
and Bloomsbury.
#ShareAStory

CELEBRATE STORIES. LOVE READING.

This book has been specially written, illustrated and published to celebrate **World Book Day.** We are a charity that offers every child and young person the opportunity to read and love books by giving you the chance to have a book of your own. To find out more, and for oodles of fun activities and reading recommendations to continue your reading journey, visit **worldbookday.com**

World Book Day in the UK and Ireland is made possible by generous sponsorship from National Book Tokens, participating publishers, booksellers, authors and illustrators. The £1* book tokens are a gift from your local bookseller.

World Book Day works in partnership with a number of charities, all of which are working to encourage a love of reading for pleasure.

The National Literacy Trust is an independent charity that encourages children and young people to enjoy reading. Just ten minutes of reading every day can make a big difference to how well you do at school and to how successful you could be in life. **literacytrust.org.uk**

The Reading Agency inspires people of all ages and backgrounds to read for pleasure and empowerment. It runs the Summer Reading Challenge in partnership with libraries; it also supports reading groups in schools and libraries all year round. Find out more and join your local library. **summerreadingchallenge.org.uk**

World Book Day also facilitates fundraising for:

Book Aid International, an international book donation and library development charity. Every year, it provides one million books to libraries and schools in communities where children would otherwise have little or no opportunity to read. **bookaid.org**

Read for Good, which motivates children in schools to read for fun through its sponsored read, which thousands of schools run on World Book Day and throughout the year. The money raised provides new books and resident storytellers in all the children's hospitals in the UK. **readforgood.org**

*€1.50 in Ireland

BAD

Mermaids

Meet the
Witches

SIBÉAL POUNDER

ILLUSTRATIONS by
Jason Cockcroft
and Laura Ellen Anderson

BLOOMSBURY
CHILDREN'S BOOKS
LONDON OXFORD NEW YORK NEW DELHI SYDNEY

MEET THE MERMAIDS ...

BEATTIE
The Hidden Lagoon's most adventurous mermaid. You'll see her driving around in her clam car or holding a pair of false teeth.

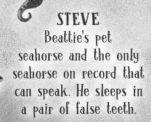

STEVE
Beattie's pet seahorse and the only seahorse on record that can speak. He sleeps in a pair of false teeth.

MIMI
Multicoloured hair and a tail to match, Mimi loves fin-fu, and Clippee, the cartoon lobster in a dress.

ZELDA
The best shockey player in the lagoon. She likes to wear her green hair in a short flick and loves a waistcoat.

AND THE WITCHES!

TIGA
The newest witch to land in Sinkville, Tiga is best known for her role in *Witch Wars*, the TV show which decides who will be Top Witch of Sinkville.

FRAN
Sinkville's most fabulous fairy. She presents *Cooking for Tiny People* and was the winner of Best and Only Fairy Film of the Year.

FLUFFANORA
The daughter of Ritzy City's most famous designer, Fluffanora is the best-dressed witch in town.

PEGGY
Sinkville's Top Witch and the kindest witch you'll meet. Terrible at spells, but an excellent friend.

For Mirabel and all the other fabulous readers who told me it might be a good idea for the witches and mermaids to finally meet ...

BLOOMSBURY CHILDREN'S BOOKS
Bloomsbury Publishing Plc
50 Bedford Square, London WC1B 3DP, UK

BLOOMSBURY, BLOOMSBURY CHILDREN'S BOOKS and the Diana logo
are trademarks of Bloomsbury Publishing Plc

First published in Great Britain in 2019 by Bloomsbury Publishing Plc

A catalogue record for this book is available from the British Library

ISBN: 978-1-5266-0453-8

2 4 6 8 10 9 7 5 3 1

Typeset by RefineCatch Limited, Bungay, Suffolk
Printed and bound in India by Thomson Press India Ltd

To find out more about our authors and books visit www.bloomsbury.com
and sign up for our newsletters

Psst!

Mermaids and Witches

Mermaids have been flopping all over this planet for as long as anyone can remember. And so have witches, only they don't flop – they cackle and they curse and THEY HAVE CATS!

Once every hundred years, the mermaids of the Hidden Lagoon and the witches of Sinkville are reunited in a famous ceremony. The Mermaid Queen travels to meet the Top Witch to celebrate the ongoing friendship between witches and mermaids everywhere.

But this time, everything is about to go magically, marvellously, megalodon-sharkally *wrong*.

Please note, all chapters in the Hidden Lagoon will be written in Mermaid. Apologies for any inconvenience caused.

 1

1

Carp!

Twottle sut CARP! Turrup zlipit con otter glup. Gree arkle no! Belfun turrup sep. Mes swottle finfin carp. Grup tap bon sentle. Finfo tinmo binboo sandbuster drip. Carp finflop grunny, you arkle starting tro get the hang fof Mermaid words!

2

Witch Day in the Hidden Lagoon

'I'VE GOT THE WITCH HATS!' Zelda roared as she swam fast through the shell-studded alleyways of Swirlyshell, knocking into clam cars and fish as she went. 'THEY ONLY HAD THREE LEFT!'

She skidded to a halt, spraying sand in Beattie and Mimi's faces.

'Mmm,' Mimi said, licking it off. 'The ketchup of the sea.'

Mimi had once spent a summer on land with legs and liked to pour sand on her hot dogs. It made her incredibly suspicious to the humans.

Zelda plonked a hat on Beattie's head.

'It looks nice with your purple hair,' Mimi said kindly. 'It reminds me of a bruised blobfish.'

Beattie stroked the hat and beamed. '*Thank you,*

4

Mimi. Ugh, I'd do *anything* to meet a Sinkville witch!'

Zelda wriggled her tail into the shell seat between them. They had got up extra early to claim seats outside the tiny Flat Crab Café, because it had the best view of the pipe Arabella Cod would take to Sinkville, the world of witches.

A mermaid with large flat-crab earrings and bright orange lipstick plonked a foam shake down in front of Zelda.

Zelda jiggled her tail, which was the most respectful way of saying thanks.

'Where's Steve?' Mimi asked.

Steve was Beattie's talking seahorse. He was the only sea creature on record that could speak.

'He's gone to make himself a witch hat.' Beattie said. 'They don't sell them in his size.'

'Why are these hats flat?' Zelda asked, as a crab scuttled up with a tray of wobbling sandbites on its back. She plucked one from the pile and chewed it. 'In all those human drawings we saw, witches wore pointy ones.'

'It's because witches are sucked up through the sink pipes if they go up to the human world,' Beattie explained. 'The suction pulls the hat into a point!'

'Look!' Mimi said, flopping over the table and spilling the foam shakes. 'The pipe. It's *glowing*.'

They looked up. The little pipe seemed to be getting brighter and brighter.

'But Arabella Cod isn't due to leave yet,' Zelda said. 'I don't think it's meant to do that.'

Beattie looked down the shell-studded street. Mermaids swam in their thousands, but no one had spotted it.

A moment later a clump of glittery dust burst from the pipe, making the fish above it scatter everywhere.

The three mermaids looked at each other, their eyes wide.

'I know …' Steve the seahorse said as he appeared in front of them, wearing a witch hat that looked like a prawn had vomited it up. 'It may be the smallest witch hat in town, but I made it, so it's definitely the most fabulous.'

Beattie pointed to the pipe. 'Steve. *Look.*'

Steve spun around just in time to see a girl with legs sinking fast.

'She fell from the pipe,' Beattie said excitedly. 'She's a witch!'

3

Mermaid Day in Sinkville

One hour earlier in Ritzy City …

Tiga skipped down the street with Fran the fabulous fairy flying beside her. Mermaid bunting and seaweed hung from the lamp posts, and bewitched fish danced above their heads.

'Mermaids are fabulous,' Fran said. 'But not as fabulous as me.'

'I've never met a mermaid!' Tiga said. 'But today is my lucky day!'

Tiga's best friend just happened to be Peggy, who was the Top Witch – and the Top Witch got to greet the Mermaid Queen! Peggy ruled all of Sinkville. She was nine going on ten. She waved to

 8

them from the steps of Linden House.

Fran groaned. 'Peggy will mess up the ceremony.'

'*Fran*,' Tiga said sternly. 'She won't mess it up.'

'Who won't mess what up?' Fluffanora asked. Her arms were weighed down with bags from Brew's, her mum's fashion boutique.

'Fran says Peggy is going to mess up the Mermaid Queen's visit,' Tiga explained.

'She probably will,' Fluffanora said. 'But in true Peggy style it'll all be OK –' She stopped and squinted at Peggy. 'Oh no, has she done that de-frizzing spell on her hair again?'

'I did that de-frizzing spell on my hair again!' Peggy shouted brightly as they all climbed the steps. 'And it didn't work … again.'

Fluffanora dragged her inside and sat her down.

Tiga ran her fingers through Peggy's gloop-covered hair.

'We'll fix this,' Fluffanora said, just as Peggy's hair whispered, 'Weeee'llll fiiiixxxx thiiiis.'

'Um, Peggy,' Tiga said, peering at her head. 'Why is your hair whispering?'

'Whhhhyyyy iiiissss yooooouuuurrrr haaaaiiiirrrr whhhhiiiisssspppppeeeeerrrriiiinnnngggg?'

'Long story,' Peggy said. 'I was running through the house doing my de-frizzing hair spell when I accidentally collided with a ghost parrot and, well –' she interlocked her fingers – 'they merged ... on my head.'

'It's fine,' Fluffanora said, spraying it with hairspray.

'Iiiitttt's ffffiiiine,' Peggy's hair repeated.

'You don't think Arabella Cod will notice?' Peggy asked hopefully.

A Linden House witch pushed a bathtub into the room.

'Ah,' Fran said, 'the bathtub is ready. We have to take it across town to collect the Mermaid Queen – she's going to pop out of one of the pipes and then we'll plonk her in the tub and push her back here.'

10

'Peggy has to get ready first,' Fluffanora said as she tipped the Brew's bags upside down and dresses tumbled out.

'I have some opinions on which outfit would be best,' Fran said, butting in. 'First we need to think about what kind of impression we want to make. For example,' she went on, holding up two dresses, 'are you a sequins witch or a lace witch?'

'I think that's the same witch,' Peggy said. 'In two different dresses. Why don't you say the magic thing that activates the pipe, while you're waiting?'

'And why is it me who has to do it?' Fran asked, knowing perfectly well why, but she liked hearing the answer.

Peggy forced a smile. 'Because only fairies can link the pipes to the Hidden Lagoon'.

Fran puffed out her chest proudly and raised her hands in the air. Glittery dust burst from her fists! She didn't notice, but it floated down and settled on the bathtub, making the plughole glow.

'Mermaids and witches are different sorts,

'*And they cannot wear certain things, like pairs of shorts,*' Fran sang in an operatic style.

'*But all that aside, we are one and the same,*

'*Mythical creatures who live down a draaaaiiiinnnn!*'

Peggy's hair whispered along with her:

'*Weeee aaaarrrreeee onnnneeee aaaannnndddd thhhheeee saaaammmmeeee.*'

Fran went black in the eyes and spun round.

'YOU ARE STEALING *MY* LINES, PEGGY'S HAIR! STOP IT RIGH—' But before she could finish, the bathtub started spinning and Fran found herself being pulled fast towards the plughole. 'Tiga!' she shouted, reaching out a tiny hand.

Tiga grabbed for her and caught hold of her beehive.

'I've got you!' Tiga said, just as her feet lifted off the floor.

The bathtub groaned and glittery dust began flowing from the plughole like water.

'WHAT'S HAAAAPPPPENNNNIIIINGGGG?' Tiga shouted as she and Fran disappeared down the plughole with a pop.

Peggy raced over and peered into the empty bathtub. 'Where did they go?'

'Thhhheeee Hiiiiddddeeeennnn Laaaagoooonnnn,' Peggy's hair whispered.

4

Beattie and Tiga Meet!

‘Are you a witch?’ Beattie whispered as Tiga floated to pavement level.

Mimi and Zelda flopped their fins around her to conceal her legs from passing mermaids.

‘What are you doing here?’ Beattie asked, but Tiga just puffed out her cheeks.

‘She can’t breathe underwater!’ Zelda cried. ‘What should we do?’

‘MAKE WAY FOR MEEEE,’ came a voice – and out of nowhere a tiny thing with a huge beehive appeared in a puff of glittery dust. She threw a clump of it at Tiga and the little witch turned into a mermaid with a shark tail.

‘Wow,’ Tiga said, taking in a deep watery breath and swishing her tail back and forth. ‘Thanks, Fran.’

 14

'You look like a mermaid from Hammerhead Heights,' Zelda said, slapping Tiga on the back. 'That's where all the mermaids with shark tails live. They have a restaurant *inside* a shark! This is Swirlyshell, the capital city of the Hidden Lagoon, and I'm Zelda, the best shockey player in town.'

'I'm Mimi,' Mimi said with an elaborate bow. 'Zelda and I are non-identical twins. I like fin-fu, talking to fish and eating the ketchup of the sea.'

Tiga looked confused.

'And I'm Beattie,' Beattie said, swimming forward and shaking Tiga's hand. 'I can't believe you're a real witch.'

'I can't believe you're a real mermaid!' Tiga said. 'I'm Tiga, and this is Fran.'

'And I'm Steve,' Steve butted in, bowing down in front of Fran. 'I'm what they call a *miracle*.'

'He's the only seahorse in the lagoon that talks,' Beattie whispered to Tiga. 'That's why he calls himself a miracle. He sleeps in a pair of false teeth.'

'And what are you?' Steve asked Fran.

'Oh, I'm *fabulous*.'

'MY QUEEN!' Steve shouted adoringly in her face.

'Well, it's nice to meet a real witch and a ...' Zelda stopped and stared at Fran. 'A *microwitch*?'

'I'm a fairy!' Fran growled.

'Well, come and join us for a foam shake,' Zelda said. 'We want to hear all about you.'

'So your best friends are Fluffanora and Peggy,' Mimi said. 'I wish they had come with you. And so does that fish next to your head who is listening in.'

The fish blinked at Tiga.

'Yes, but Peggy is the Top Witch,' Tiga explained. 'So she couldn't have come because she'll be the witch greeting your queen. I'd really better go soon. I have to present Arabella Cod with this –' she held up a soggy clump of cat hair – 'it's a hair sculpture that's supposed to look like a mermaid.'

Zelda raised an eyebrow. 'Witches are *weird*.'

A flubbery rumble echoed through the sunken

streets as hundreds of mermaids swam fast towards the palace.

'It's time,' Zelda said with a nod, just as Arabella Cod swam to the gates. She was festooned in jewellery from all the different cities in the lagoon – bright red and purple beads for Lobstertown, shells for Swirlyshell, a sharp triangle crown for Hammerhead Heights, chunky cool blue gems for Anchor Rock and pink crystals for Oysterdale. The crowds erupted into cheers!

'She looks expensive,' Fran said.

Tiga tried to stand up and flopped on to the table. 'Well, I'd better go. I can't let Peggy down – my *only* job was to present this … special gift at the end of the ceremony.'

They all stared at the ball of hair.

'It'll go nicely with all the queen's expensive jewellery,' Fran said, before mouthing to Steve, 'IT WON'T.'

Tiga hugged Beattie and slapped tails with Mimi and Zelda. 'Maybe one day we'll meet again!'

Arabella Cod made for the pipe and waved goodbye as the crowds cheered.

Tiga hastily started swimming. 'We'd better go, Fran!'

The queen vanished with a pop.

'Not so fast, Tiga,' Fran said quietly. She waved her hand, making Tiga crash-land back in her chair.

'SILENCE FOR MY QUEEN!' Steve cried.

'The queen is in the pipe,' Zelda pointed out.

'*This* queen,' Steve said, pointing his snout at Fran.

Fran pirouetted on his false teeth. 'I'm afraid we can't use the pipe to get back, not while Arabella Cod is up there.'

'Why?' Tiga said, her eyes wide.

'Because that pipe operates a one-up-at-a-time policy. You can't go up it until Arabella Cod comes back.'

'So what are we going to do?' Tiga cried, waving the ball of soggy hair in Fran's face.

'Well, for starters, we aren't going to wave a terrible hairstyle in my face. And secondly, we'll find a bathtub. That's how we got here, so that's how we'll get back.'

 18

Tiga turned to Beattie. 'Do you have a bathtub?'

Beattie shook her head. 'I'm afraid not, that's a human thing. But wait! I know where we can get one – there's one for sale in Sandbury's department store. It's always in the window!'

They swam fast, weaving between sea creatures and mermaids driving giant clam cars. A mermaid honked her horn as Tiga darted out from one of the rocky passageways on Mottleton Alley.

'WATCH WHERE YOU'RE GOING, SHARKY!'

Beattie watched Tiga try to control her tail. She wobbled left and then right, steadying herself just in time to bang into a seal.

'The witch is getting the hang of the shark tail!' Zelda cheered.

They screeched to a halt outside Sandbury's. Beattie's eyes grew wide.

'NO!' Zelda cried, sliding her nose down the glass.

'Oh will you look at that,' Mimi said cheerily. 'That's a big problem, isn't it … ?'

5

Expensive Bathtub

They all stared at the bathtub in the window of Sandbury's. The cave window was peppered with shells, and the bath was filled with seaweed. An ornamental octopus lazed in it, waving the price tag.

'HOW MUCH?' Zelda cried.

'Is a million sharpits a lot of money?' Tiga asked.

'Nobody panic,' Fran said. 'We can just go inside and quickly *use* the bathtub. I just need a few seconds to work my magic.'

Inside the door, a mermaid wearing a swirly Sandbury's hat greeted them. 'Which department, please?'

'Bathtubs,' Zelda said.

'Ah,' he said. 'You mean Sunken Human Treasures.' A pod of green Sandbury's dolphin assistants appeared pulling a shell-studded sleigh.

They hopped in.

'This is amazing,' Tiga said as she patted a dolphin.

'Go straight, through the make-up department, past clam-car accessories and you'll see a wall of sunken human shoes. The bathtub – only one remaining – is on the left.'

He whistled and the dolphins shot off, pulling them past mermaids being pampered by pufferfish in the make-up section, through the clam-car-accessories section, where a mermaid was buying a bumper sticker that read HONK IF YOU'RE A SEAL THAT CAN READ, before finally grinding to a halt by a wall of a thousand shoes. The octopus in the bathtub rose up high on its legs and waved a tentacle in Fran's face.

'Ah,' Mimi said. 'He says he heard what you said outside. No magic. If we want to use it, we have to buy it before we use it. It's store policy.'

Tiga looked at her curiously. 'Are you sure that's what he said?'

The octopus began madly waving its tentacles.

'Mmm-hmm,' Mimi said, taking it all in. She turned

21

to the others. 'That's what he said, but I'm not going to repeat that last bit because he is a very *rude* octopus.'

'Can't you just do some quick magic?' Tiga muttered to Fran. 'We only need the tub for a second.'

Fran clutched her heart. 'Tiga, do you *know* what would happen to me if I committed a crime in mermaid territory?'

Tiga looked around. 'You'd be told off?'

'Viperview,' Fran said with a shiver.

'Oh yeah,' Zelda said. 'We have an amazing prison.'

'It's guarded by evil dolphins,' Fran said, grabbing Tiga by the collar. 'The worst kind of dolphin!'

'Nobody panic,' Beattie said. 'We just need to miraculously find another bathtub. Any ideas where we'd find one?'

They all floated on the spot, thinking. Mimi tried some shoes on her hands.

The ground rumbled as a giant fake prawn floated past the window.

'IT'S TIME TO COUTURE THAT CRUSTACEAN!' boomed a voice from within it.

'What's that?' Tiga said as colourful lights danced across the store and music began blasting.

'Oh, that's just *Catwalk Prawn*,' Beattie said. 'It's a game show. They're looking for contestants, and if you win you get –' Beattie stopped and her eyes grew wide.

'COME ON!' she shouted. 'WE NEED TO COUTURE A CRUSTACEAN!'

6

Catwalk Prawn!

Inside the giant floating fake prawn was a TV set unlike anything Tiga had seen before.

'It's not as good as the set of my TV show, *Cooking for Tiny People*,' Fran said.

Tiga noticed Fran was now wearing a pair of swimming goggles, complete with little glittery windscreen wipers that squeaked back and forth.

'Um ... Fran, what's on your face?'

'What a silly question!' Fran cried. 'Eyes. Nose. Mouth. Main face meat. The eyebrow twins.'

'The winner of *Catwalk Prawn* gets a voucher to spend in Sandbury's department store,' Beattie explained. 'It's a voucher to use on one thing – we could get the bathtub! We just have to win.'

'Do we have enough time?' Tiga said, glancing at

her watch. It was soggy and the little witch-shaped hands were wringing out their hair. 'I don't even know what time it is. My watch is busy drying its hair.'

'IN CELEBRATION OF TODAY'S CEREMONY WITH THE WITCHES, *CATWALK PRAWN* IS WIIIITTTTCCCCH THEEEEMED!' squealed the presenter. She had inky blue hair and wore a shell top with goldfish-bowl shoulders. Her tail was covered in strings of pearls and she'd painted prawn patterns up her arms. 'I'm your host, Rara Crispy, and WELCOME to … *CATWALK PRAWN!*'

The crowd went wild.

Zelda high-fived Tiga. 'Who better to win a witch-themed competition than a *witch*.'

'There will be three fabulous rounds!' Rara Crispy cried. 'Three chances to WOW us with your prawniest skills. You'll need to impress our judges! First we have Figgy Bass, our most famous designer!'

A mermaid in a sparkling green top and headscarf to match swam onstage to much applause.

Fran and Steve cheered, doing somersaults in excitement.

'I love her,' Steve whispered to Fran. 'She has a special jellyfish that only exists to comb her eyelashes.'

'And our second judge ... owner of Sandbury's and inventor of the octopus moustache ... IT'S WIGBERT KRILL!'

A bunch of seals clapped loudly in the corner. Wigbert Krill insisted they be there. It made him feel important.

'BUT,' Rara Crispy went on, 'a show is not a show without contestants!'

The lights flashed across the audience and halted above the head of a mermaid in a lobster hat.

She swam up to the stage as the crowd clapped their tails and hands.

'I'm Opal Eelworth,' the mermaid said. 'I'm eleven and I'm from Lobstertown.'

Beattie sank in her seat. 'Lobstertown is really cool,' she whispered to Tiga. 'And Figgy Bass *always* wants the mermaids from Lobstertown to win, because that's where she's from. She's completely biased.'

The lights flashed again.

'Quick,' Beattie said, nudging Tiga around the audience, trying to keep up with the lights.

They stopped above Beattie.

'YES!' she roared. 'My name is Beattie and I'm from Swirlyshell.' She gave Tiga the thumbs up.

The crowd cheered and the lights began to flash once more. This time, they fell on Tiga!

Tiga felt herself going bright red. 'Um … I'm Tiga and I'm from –'

She looked to Fran, who was mouthing 'showbiz smile', which wasn't helpful at all.

The crowd stared.

'HAMMERHEAD HEIGHTS!' Zelda called out. 'SHE'S FROM HAMMERHEAD HEIGHTS!'

'Ah,' Rara said. 'So we have Opal, Beattie, Tiga and –' she stared at Zelda – 'you.'

'Oh no,' Zelda said, backing away. 'I'm not good at—'

27

'WE HAVE OUR FOUR CONTESTANTS!' Rara Crispy roared.

The crowd went wild!

'One of you,' Rara Crispy oozed, 'will win a voucher for Sandbury's, a couture outfit designed by Figgy Bass and the We Adore Your Prawn trophy!'

Beattie laughed. 'This will be easy. All we have to do is beat Opal Eelworth. You'll be home in no time!'

Mimi pushed her way through the audience and floated right at the front.

Octopuses danced down the catwalk. Four shell-shaped tables with treasure chests lined each side.

The contestants took their places.

'What is all this stuff?' Tiga whispered to Beattie as she swam over her table and peered inside the chests.

'It's the things you use to make tiny outfits for the prawns. Then they walk down the catwalk to be judged.'

On each table sat a prawn.

Tiga's stared up at her.

'That prawn doesn't like me,' Fran whispered from where she was hiding in the treasure chest.

28

'It's a *prawn* Fran,' Tiga said. 'They don't have emotions or opinions.'

Steve popped up next to Fran. 'Prawns have *lots* of opinions, Tiga. And at least two emotions.'

Beattie glanced across at Zelda who was stationed next to Opal Eelworth. Her prawn was biting her finger.

'YOUR FIRST CHALLENGE IS TO CREATE THE ICONIC WITCH ACCESSORY – A FLAT AND FABULOUS HAT! You can use any of the items in your treasure chest, and you have five minutes!'

'Good luck,' Beattie whispered to Tiga.

The cameras rolled. An octopus counted down on his tentacles. But he only got down to three.

'TWO! ONE!' Rara Crispy finished. 'COUTURE THAT CRUSTACEAN!'

Tiga reached a hand into her treasure chest and hit something slimy. She pulled out some seaweed and began cutting it.

'I wish Fluffanora was here,' she whispered to Beattie. 'She'd be so good at this.'

Beattie dived into her treasure chest and emerged with a black eye.

'Beattie, your eye!' Zelda cried.

'I think there's rocks in there,' Beattie said, hitting the treasure chest with her tail.

Five minutes dribbled past far too quickly.

'PUT YOUR PRAWNS DOWN!' Rara Crispy cried.

Beattie grabbed a flat fish and plonked it on her prawn's head.

The lights swivelled from the contestants to the catwalk. A mermaid band with dolphin tails and sequinned hats began clashing shells together.

Beattie, Zelda and Tiga linked arms as they watched their prawns make their way down the catwalk.

Tiga had gone for a classic wide-brimmed design made of seaweed and sparkly black rocks. She'd added a sprinkle of sand for texture.

Zelda had gone for full colour with multicoloured shells and purple sea flowers.

Opal's … didn't seem to be wearing a hat at all.

 30

'Your prawn doesn't have a witch hat,' Zelda said.

Opal scrunched up her face. 'Yes it does, amateur. It's wearing a *grain-of-sand hat*, duh.'

'Opal will definitely be kicked off first,' Beattie whispered. 'That means we win no matter what. We're all on the same team. Team *Bathtub*.'

Tiga laughed and squeezed Beattie's arm.

Rara Crispy floated over to the judges.

'Judges! You have a tough decision to make.'

There was a weird crunching noise.

They all looked to the catwalk.

Beattie's prawn had vanished, but the fish hat it had been wearing was suddenly awake ... and it looked fatter.

Mimi slapped her hand to her head. 'The fish ate Beattie's prawn.'

'Spit him out,' Beattie pleaded. 'You're meant to be the *hat*.'

Wigbert Krill's octopus moustache wiggled. 'A hat is not a hat if it eats you. And so I'm afraid, Beattie – you GAAAAWWWWN!'

A chunky octopus appeared behind Beattie, picked her up and placed her with a thud on her shell table and hoisted it in the air – ceremoniously swimming her around the room while everyone clapped.

'The rest of you,' Rara Crispy said grandly, 'live to prawn another day!'

'Well,' Mimi said cheerily, 'at least Beattie got a black eye. She's not leaving with nothing.'

And then there were three.

7

No Prawn, You GAAAAWWWWN!

The next round was tights, because witches like to wear ones that have fun patterns.

'HOW DO YOU MAKE TIGHTS FOR A PRAWN?!' Tiga had cried when the round began. Now Beattie and Mimi were watching the prawns make their way down the catwalk.

'Tiga's done a really good job,' Beattie whispered. 'She's made tights for each tiny leg.'

Mimi pointed at Opal's design. 'There's no tights on that one at all!'

'Um, they're *invisible* tights,' Opal said, crossing her arms.

'That's cheating,' Mimi said, but Opal just smirked and looked away.

Zelda's prawn floated off and left the building.

Beattie put her head in her hands.

'What?' Tiga whispered over to her. 'What's wrong?'

'AH!' Rara Crispy shouted when she spotted it. The lights went out, the octopus lolloped over and grabbed Zelda.

'I'm afraid the rules state that if your prawn swims off, you are out,' Rara Crispy said, swimming about the audience. 'Because—'

'NO PRAWN, YOU GAAAAWWWWN!' the crowd cheered.

The octopus launched Zelda across the room and out of the door.

'So unfair!' Zelda huffed.

'I think Opal is going to win this,' Figgy Bass said. 'I just love the invisible tights – and that grain-of-sand hat was like nothing I've ever seen before – because I literally couldn't see it!'

'Tiga *has* to win this,' Beattie whispered, as the lights rolled around the room and the final round began. 'We need to stop Opal from winning. She's cheating. So why don't we cheat too?'

'But we're not cheaters,' Mimi said.

Steve floated next to Beattie's ear. 'Say the word and I can strike. A seahorse tail up the snotter and Opal will be out of action.'

'We're not attacking a mermaid to win a game show,' Beattie said.

'AND NOW THE PRAWNS WILL TAKE TO THE CATWALK FOR THE FINAL TIME!' Rara Crispy cheered. 'Let's see the capes!'

'WHY DO THE ROUNDS GO SO QUICKLY?!' Zelda roared.

Opal Eelworth's prawn floated down the catwalk. 'It's an invisible cape,' she said, to much applause.

Beattie scrunched up her fist and shattered a rock she was squeezing. 'She's cheating *so much*.'

Tiga's prawn followed in a beautiful shell cape that she'd woven into a cool W shape. 'W for witch,' Tiga said.

'I love the invisible one,' Figgy Bass said with a smile.

'Opal's going to win,' Zelda groaned. 'So unfair.'

'Fran,' Beattie whispered across the stage. 'Fran … are you sleeping. Fran?! Can you do some magic

35

to help? Pssst, Fran! HELP.'

Fran woke with a snort, cuddling Peggy's weird cat-hair present.

'YEULCH!' she gagged, launching it across the set. It landed on Tiga's prawn, covering it completely.

'I didn't mean do *that*,' Beattie said.

The prawn's head popped out of the clump of cat hair and continued down the catwalk like nothing had happened.

'And now it's time for the final result,' Rara Crispy shouted. 'Judges, over to you.'

Wigbert Krill spotted the hairy prawn. 'Do you know what I hate?'

'Dolphin squeaks?' Fran guessed. 'Tuna dancing? Seal eyelashes? Strange-shaped rocks? Jelly elbows? Hair knots? Arrogant turtles? Oxygen?'

'Who is this?' Wigbert Krill said, prodding Fran's beehive with his finger.

Tiga drew a breath. 'Oh frogs, he touched her hair …'

'JUST TELL US WHO'S WON!' Fran roared in his face.

'Well,' Wigbert Krill said, wiping away the fairy spit. 'I was about to say I hate any design that doesn't involve creative hair. I LOVE creative hair, it's why I invented the octopus moustache. And Tiga's prawn … well, that's some creative hair.'

'WHAT?' Opal Eelworth cried. 'MINE HAS CREATIVE HAIR TOO! INVISIBLE CREATIVE HAIR!'

'Tiga! Tiga! Tiga!' the crowd chanted.

Wigbert Krill whispered something to Figgy Bass. She nodded reluctantly and handed Rara Crispy a slither of seaweed with the winner's name.

'And so, the mermaid taking home the Sandbury's voucher, couture outfit and We Adore Your Prawn trophy is …' Rara Crispy teased. 'TIGA!'

Beattie, Mimi and Zelda leaped out of their seats and linked arms with Tiga. They swam up high, shouting, 'BATHTUB! BATHTUB! BATHTUB!'

Suddenly Tiga stopped, remembering why they were there.

'Oh no,' she said. 'We're almost out of time.'

8

Fran Shows Off

Beattie pushed and Tiga pulled until the bathtub was safely down a quiet side street.

'Here,' Beattie said, handing Tiga a little shell box. 'One for you and each of your friends – Fluffanora and …'

'Peggy,' Tiga said with a smile as she snapped open the box. Inside were three mood rings.

Zelda slapped Tiga on the back. 'You're not bad, Tiga. I know we're going to meet again. Maybe next time we can play a round of shockey.'

Fran shot some glittery dust at Tiga's new ring. 'Now Tiga can always come back. All she needs to do is rub the ring and she'll morph into a mermaid!'

They all swam closer and peered into the ring. A little mermaid with a shark tail swam around inside it.

Steve bowed in front of Fran. 'Nice to meet you, and your hair, Queen.'

Fran raised her arms as she landed on the edge of the bathtub. 'I will connect our worlds and whisk us magically home! *Mermaids and witches are different sorts, and they cannot wear certain things like pairs of shor—*'

A giant megalodon shark came crashing down the alleyway, covered in fairy lights and a sign that flashed JAWELLAS.

'That's the shark restaurant from Hammerhead Heights I was telling you about!' Zelda said.

Tiga caught sight of mermaids beyond its teeth, dining at grand tables. It squeezed its way down the alleyway, knocking shells off the wall as it went.

'WELL, THAT MESSED EVERYTHING UP,' came a furious fairy voice.

They peered into the bathtub to see Fran lying like a starfish on top of a rumbling plughole.

'Not again,' Tiga groaned.

'WHAT'S HAPPENING?!' Beattie cried as she was sucked tail-first to Sinkville.

9

Witch Tails

Arabella Cod was propelled out of the bath and splatted into the wall as Beattie, Steve, Tiga and Fran popped out of the plughole in a cloud of glittery dust.

Witches rushed to peel the Mermaid Queen off the wall. One shell-shocked witch scraped glitter off her tongue.

'Hello,' Tiga whispered sheepishly to Peggy, as she and Beattie peeked out of the bathtub.

'DY-ING,' Steve rasped. 'DY-ING.'

Fluffanora plucked him from the tub and dunked him in her Clutterbucks cocktail before anyone noticed.

'I can fix this,' Peggy whispered, flicking her finger. 'I'll give them legs.'

There was a popping sound. Tiga looked down – she still had a tail!

 40

'Ugh,' Peggy groaned, trying to steady her new giant lobster tail. 'I'm so bad at spells!'

'I HAVE A TAIL!' a witch shouted.

'I'M SLIMING EVERYWHERE!' shouted another.

Peggy stared at her finger. 'That spell went so wrong.'

Arabella Cod slid down the wall and slopped on to the floor. She looked up to see all the tails waving in the air. 'Oh … you made yourselves into mermaids to honour me! And you're all waving THANK YOU with your tails!'

'We are?' a witch muttered to another.

'YES!' Peggy shouted as she flopped into a lamp and knocked it over. 'THAT IS EXACTLY WHAT THIS IS. *EXACTLY!*'

Fran floated past with a seahorse tail and plucked Steve from Fluffanora's cocktail. She placed him gently in Beattie's hand. 'Goodbye, *miracle.*'

Beattie squeezed Tiga one last time and with a wave of Fran's hand, some very quick muttering, and an efficient pop, they vanished down the plughole.

Fran clicked her fingers and the witches' tails snapped back to legs.

'I couldn't think of a more perfect gift,' Arabella Cod said as Peggy lifted the queen and heaved her back into the bathtub. 'I can't wait to tell my lagoon about the most magical Top Witch to ever rule Sinkville! And I agree with you, Peggy, we should change the rules and visit each other more frequently than just every one hundred years! Goodbye, witchy friends, I shall see you soon! Goodbye!'

With a final flick of the tail, she disappeared down the plughole.

'Oh no!' Tiga cried, holding up a soggy mass of hair. 'Peggy, after all that I forgot to give her the cat-hair sculpture!'

'I think the tails were a much better present,' Peggy said with a smile.

'Thhhhaaaattttt haaaaiiiirrrr iiiissss hooooorrrriiiibbbblllleeee,' Peggy's hair whispered.

'Dive into a fin-tastic, madcap adventure that's funnier than being tickled by a giant octopus!'

Award-winning author David Solomons on *Bad Mermaids*

 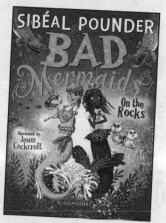

AVAILABLE NOW

And look out for

BAD Mermaids
On Thin Ice

COMING SOON!

WORLD **BOOK** DAY

SHARE A STORY

Well **hello** there! We are

Overjoyed that you have **joined our celebration** of

Reading books and **sharing stories**, because we

Love bringing **books** to you.

Did you know, we are a **charity** dedicated to celebrating the

Brilliance of **reading for pleasure** for everyone, everywhere?

Our mission is to help you discover **brand new stories** and

Open your mind to exciting **new worlds** and **characters**, from

Kings and **queens** to **wizards** and **pirates** to **animals** and **adventurers** and so many more. We couldn't

Do it without all the amazing **authors** and **illustrators**, **booksellers** and **bookshops**, **publishers**, schools and **libraries** out there –

And most importantly, we couldn't do it all without . . .

YOU!

On your bookmarks, get set, READ! Happy Reading. Happy World Book Day.

Illustrations © Rob Biddulph

Read on for a sneak peek at
the first book in Sibéal Pounder's
WiTCH WARS series

AVAILABLE NOW!

1

Down the Plughole

It would have been very difficult to spot Fran the fairy on the day this story begins. Her dress may have been puffy, her hair may have been huge, but she was barely the size of a small potato.

Fran was slowly sidestepping across a garden lawn, holding a large, limp leaf in front of her. She didn't want the owner of the garden to see her because Miss Heks was a terrible old woman with a grim face and size eleven shoes. If she had seen Fran she would've squashed her immediately.

Fran and her leaf were on a mission. There was something very important in the shed at the bottom of Miss Heks's garden. That something was a girl called Tiga Whicabim.

☆⭐☆

'You!' Tiga said, pointing at a slug that was sliding its way across an old stone sink. 'You will be the star of my show! You will play the role of Beryl, an ambitious dancer with severe hiccups.'

Tiga had been in the shed for hours. The evil Miss Heks had been her guardian for as long as Tiga could remember and she had quickly learned to keep out of her way. If she didn't, the old bat would make her sew up the holes in her disgusting, scratchy dresses. Or she would force Tiga to run up and down the garden in her gigantic, ugly shoes, bellowing things like 'FASTER!' and 'OH, DID YOU TRIP?' from the kitchen window.

Tiga shone a torch on the slug.

'You are going to be the best actor the world has ever seen!' she cried.

Fran sighed when she saw that.

Not because she'd finally found Tiga, after a long and perilous journey that had almost ended with her being eaten by a dog.

No, the reason Fran sighed was because she loved a bit of acting!

Despite her small size, Fran was a big deal in the world of show business. Everyone called her Fran the Fabulous Fairy (a name she had made up for herself). She had hosted many award-winning TV shows like *Cooking for Tiny People* and *The Squashed and the Swatted* and she'd played the lead role in *Glittery Sue* – a tragic drama about a small lady called Sue who got some glitter in her hair and couldn't get it out again.

'An actor you say!' Fran said, making Tiga jump.

Tiga stared, mouth open, at the small person that marched across the shed and – very ungracefully, and with much grunting – climbed up the leg of her trusty old rocking chair.

Fran stretched out a hand.

'Very delighted to meet you, Tiga! Now, it's pronounced *Teega*, isn't it? That's what I thought! I'm very good at names and absolutely everything else. I'm Fran the Fabulous Fairy. But you can call me Fran. Or Fabulous. BUT NEVER JUST FAIRY. I hate that.'

Tiga, understandably, assumed she had gone mad. Or at the very least fallen asleep.

She squinted at the little thing with big hair and then looked to the slug for reassurance, but it was sliding its way across the floor as if it knew exactly who Fran was, and was trying to escape.

'I don't think,' Fran said, pointing at the slug, 'that she should be acting in the lead role. She is slimy and not paying much attention.'

Fran wiggled a foot and a beehive of hair just like her own appeared on top of the slug's head.

'Much, much, *much* better,' she said.

Tiga panicked – the slug had *hair*! Not any old hair, a beehive of perfectly groomed hair! It was a split-second reaction, but with a flick of her hand she batted the fairy clean off the rocking chair.

Fran wobbled from left to right and tried to steady herself.

'Did you just *swat* me?' she snapped. 'The ultimate insult!'

Tiga tried to avoid eye contact and instead looked at

the slug. She couldn't be sure, but it looked a lot like it was shaking its head at her.

'WITCHES ARE NOT ALLOWED TO SWAT FAIRIES. IT IS THE LAW,' Fran ranted.

'I'm sorry!' Tiga cried. 'I didn't think you were real – I thought you were just my imagination! You don't need to call me a witch.'

'Yes I do,' said Fran, floating in front of Tiga with her hands on her hips. 'Because you are one.'

'I am one what?' Tiga asked.

'One witch,' said Fran as she twirled in the air, got her puffy dress caught in her wings and crash-landed on the floor.

'BRAAAAT!' came a bellow from across the garden. 'Time to leave the shed. Your dinner is ready!'

Tiga glanced nervously out of the window. 'If you are real, although I'm still not convinced you are, you'd better leave now. Miss Heks is a terrible old woman and she will do horrible, nasty, ear-pinching things to you.'

Fran ignored her and went back to twirling in the air. 'What are you having for dinner?'

'Cheese water,' Tiga said with a sigh. 'It's only ever cheese water.'

Fran thought about this for a moment. 'And how do you make this cheese water?'

'You find a bit of mouldy old cheese and you put it in some boiling water,' said Tiga, looking ill.

Fran swooped down lower and landed on the sink. 'Well, I'm afraid we don't have cheese water in Ritzy City – it's mostly cakes.'

Tiga stared at the fairy. 'Ritzy where?'

'*Riiiitzzzzzy Ciiiiity!*' Fran cheered, waving her hands in the air.

Tiga shrugged. 'Never heard of it.'

'But you're a witch,' said Fran.

'I am not a witch!' Tiga cried.

'You SO are!'

'I am not!'

'Definitely are,' said Fran, nodding her head. 'Even your name says so.'

And with that she flicked her tiny finger, sending a burst of glittery dust sailing across the room.

TIGA WHICABIM, the dust read.

Then it began to wobble and rearrange itself into something new.

I AM A BIG WITCH.

'You've cheated somehow,' Tiga mumbled, moving the dust letters about in the air. Most people would've believed Fran by this point, but Tiga wasn't used to magic and fun and insane fairies. So, despite this very convincing evidence that she might just be a witch, Tiga still walked towards the door. Towards the cheese water.

'TIGA!' bellowed Miss Heks. 'YOUR CHEESE WATER HAS REACHED BOILING POINT.'

'Cheese water,' Fran chuckled. 'Wait! Where are you going, Tiga?'

'To eat dinner,' said Tiga. 'Bye, Fabulous Fairy Fran. It was lovely to meet you.'

Fran raised a hand in the air. 'Wait! *What?* You're not coming with me to Ritzy City, a place of wonder and absolutely no cheese?'

Tiga paused. Even if it was a mad dream, it was better than cheese water. She turned on her heel and walked back towards Fran.

Fran squealed and squeaked and did somersaults in the air.

'WHAT'S GOING ON IN THERE? I KNOW YOU CAN HEAR ME, YOU LITTLE MAGGOT!' Miss Heks shouted.

Tiga could see Miss Heks stomping her way towards the shed.

'Quick!' Fran cried. 'We must go to Ritzy City right now!'

'*How?*' Tiga cried, frantically looking around the shed for an escape route.

'Down the sink pipes, of course,' Fran said as she shot through the air and straight down the plughole.

'Come on, Tiga!' her shrill little voice echoed from somewhere inside the sink.

Tiga leaned over the stone sink and stared down the plughole.

There was nothing down there. No light. And certainly no city, that was for sure.

The door to the shed flew open and splinters of old wood went soaring through the air.

'WHAT IS GOING ON?' Miss Heks bellowed.

'NOW!' Fran yelled.

Tiga wiggled a finger in the plughole.

This is nonsense, she thought, just as she disappeared.

Aventurine is the fiercest dragon in the mountains. But what happens when she is tricked into drinking enchanted chocolate and becomes ... a HUMAN?

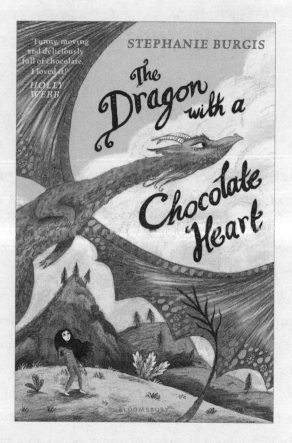

Read on for a taste of this delicious adventure!

AVAILABLE NOW

CHAPTER 1

I can't say I ever wondered what it felt like to be human. But then, my grandfather Grenat always said, 'It's *safer not to talk to your food*' – and as every dragon knows, humans are the most dangerous kind of meal there is.

Of course, as a young dragon, all I ever saw of them were their jewels and their books. The jewels were delightful, but their books were just maddening. What a waste of ink! No matter how hard I squinted, I could never make it past the first few paragraphs of cramped, crabby text. The last time I tried, I got so frustrated I burned three of those books to cinders with angry puffs of my breath.

'Don't you have any higher feelings?' my brother demanded, when he saw what I'd done. Jasper wanted to be a philosopher, so he always tried to stay calm, but his tail began to lash dangerously, sending gold coins showering through our cavern as he glared at the smoking pile before me. 'Just think,' he told me. 'Every one of those books was written by a creature whose brain was half the size of one of your forefeet. And yet, apparently, even *they* have more patience than you!'

'Oh, really?' I loved goading high-minded Jasper into losing his temper ... and now that I'd laid waste to my tiny paper enemies, I was ready for fun. So I braced myself, scales rippling with secret delight, and said, 'Well, I think anyone who wants to spend his time reading ant scribbles must have an ant-sized brain himself.'

'Arrrrgh!'

He let out the most satisfying roar of rage and leaped forward, landing exactly where I'd been sitting only a moment ago. If I hadn't been expecting it, I would have been slammed into a mountain of loose diamonds and emeralds, and my still-soft scales would have been bruised all over. But Jasper was the one who landed there instead, while I joyously pounced on his back and rubbed his snout in the pile of rocks.

'Children!' Our mother raised her head from her forefeet and let out a long-suffering snort that blew through the cave, sending more gold coins flying. 'Some of us are trying to sleep after a long, hard hunt!'

'I would have helped you hunt,' I said, jumping off Jasper. 'If you'd let me come –'

'Your scales haven't hardened enough to withstand even a wolf's bite.' Mother's great head sank back down towards her glittering blue-and-gold feet. 'Let alone a bullet or a mage's spell,' she added wearily. 'In another thirty years, perhaps, when you're nearly grown and ready to fly ...'

'I can't wait another thirty *years*!' I bellowed. My voice echoed around the cave, until Grandfather and both of my aunts were calling their own sleepy protests down the long tunnels of our home, but I ignored them. 'I can't live cooped up in this mountain forever, going nowhere, doing nothing –'

'*Jasper* is using his quiet years to teach himself philosophy.' Mother's voice no longer sounded weary;

it grew cold and hard, like a diamond, as her neck stretched higher and higher above me, her giant golden eyes narrowing into dangerous slits focused solely on me, her disobedient daughter. 'Other dragons have found their own passions in literature, history or mathematics. Tell me, Aventurine: have you managed to find *your* passion yet?'

I ground my teeth together and scratched my front right claws through the piled gold beneath my feet. 'Lessons are boring. I want to explore and –'

'And how, exactly, do you plan to communicate with the creatures you meet on your explorations?' Mother asked sweetly. 'Or have you been progressing further with your language studies than I had imagined?'

Jasper let out a muffled snicker behind me. I swung around and shot a ball of smoke at him. He let it explode harmlessly in his face, his eyes gleaming with amusement.

'I can speak six languages already,' I muttered as I turned back to Mother.

Still, I couldn't quite lift my head to meet her gaze.

'By the time she was your age,' Mother said, 'your

sister could speak and write twenty.'

'Hmmph.'

I didn't dare snort smoke at Mother. But I would have snorted it at Citrine if she had been stuck here with us, instead of living far away in her perfectly extraordinary, one-of-a-kind, dragon-sized palace. Citrine wrote epic poetry that filled other dragons with awe and was worshipped like a queen by every creature who came near her.

No one could measure up to my older sister. There was no point even trying.

I could feel Mother's gaze on me grow even sharper, as if she'd read my thoughts. 'Language,' she said, quoting one of Jasper's favourite philosophers, 'is a dragon's greatest power, reaching far beyond the realm of tooth and claw.'

'I know,' I muttered.

'Do you really, Aventurine?' Her long neck curved as her massive head swung down to look me in the eyes. 'Because courage is one thing, but reck-lessness is quite another. You may think yourself a ferocious beast, but outside this mountain you wouldn't survive a day. So you had better start being grateful that you have older and wiser relatives to look after you.'

Mother was sleeping deeply only two minutes later, her heavy breaths *whoosh*ing as calmly and evenly through the cavern as if we'd never even had an argument.

'Not a day?' Jasper whispered, once she was safely asleep. He shook off the last of the gemstones clinging to his back, and grinned at me, showing all of his teeth. 'Not an hour, more likely. Not even half an hour, knowing you.'

I glared at him, mantling my wings. 'I could look after myself perfectly well. I'm bigger and fiercer than anything else in these mountains.'

'But are you smarter?' He snorted. 'I'd wager all the gold in this cavern that even wolves are better at philosophical debates than you. And they probably don't set things on fire every time they lose!'

'Ohhh!' I whirled around, lashing my tail. But there was no escape. The cavern walls were too close, and feeling closer with every second. They were pushing in around me until I could barely breathe.

And I was supposed to spend another thirty years trapped inside this mountain, listening to my relatives tell me off for the fact that it was boring?

Never.

That was when I realised exactly what I had to do.

But I wasn't stupid, no matter what anyone thought. So I waited until Jasper finally gave up teasing me and curled up with one of his new human books – one that I hadn't burned. It was a philosophical tract, so I knew I would be safe.

'I'm going on a walk through the tunnels,' I told him, when he had flicked the pages five times with his claw.

'Mm-hmm,' Jasper murmured, without looking up. 'Aventurine, listen to this: this fellow thinks it's morally wrong to eat meat. *And* fish, too! He won't hurt any breathing creatures, so he only eats plants. Isn't that fascinating?'

'*Fascinating?* He's going to starve!' I flicked my ears in horror. 'I told you humans had pebbles for brains!'

But my brother didn't even hear me. Smoke trickled in a long, happy stream through his nostrils as he held the tiny book close to his eyes, rumbling with satisfaction.

I stepped right over his tail, one foot after another, on my way to freedom.

Rattling snores echoed down the long tunnels from the caverns where Grandfather Grenat, Aunt Tourmaline and Aunt Émeraude slept. Luckily, at this time of day, when the sun was at its highest, no one was likely to wake at a few scrabbling sounds from the corners of the mountain. Dropping to my belly, I wriggled my way up the side tunnel I'd discovered two years earlier, the one that was too small for any of the grown-ups to use. At the very top, filled and hidden by a boulder the size of my head, was a secret entrance to the mountain. It was my favourite spot in the world.

I'd shown Jasper of course, ages ago, but he almost never visited it – only when I dragged him there. He was always happiest curled up in our cavern with a book, or scratching out long, wordy treatises with one foreclaw dipped in ink.

I was the one who loved pushing the boulder free and poking the tip of my snout out of the hole, to take deep, tingling breaths of the fresh, outside air and watch the clouds float through the sky overhead. I'd never dared to go any further, but I lay there for hours sometimes, just dreaming of the day when I would finally be allowed to stretch my wings and fly across the endless sky.

Today, for the first time ever, I wasn't going to stop at dreaming.

I was going to show Jasper – *and* Mother – just how capable I was of taking care of myself. Then the grown-ups would have no excuse to keep me hidden away any longer.

With exhilaration flooding through me, I folded my wings tightly against my sides and lunged for the outside world and freedom.

It was harder than I'd expected to squeeze out of the hole. My shoulders stuck in the opening until I nearly roared with effort. I had to bite my mouth shut and swallow down choking smoke to keep myself silent. Finally, *finally*, I forced myself free with an explosive *pop!* It sent me tumbling on to the ground outside ... and whimpering with pain. My folded wings had scraped so hard against the rough, craggy edges of the rocks that there were ragged tears, now, in my silver and crimson scales.

What had Mother said? *'Your scales haven't hardened enough to withstand even a wolf's bite ...'*

I gnashed my teeth and pushed myself up on to all four feet, babying my wings by holding them half folded at my side. Every breeze that blew across them made me wince, but I growled away the pain.

So, I wouldn't be making my first attempt at flight today. Never mind. I didn't need to fly to catch my prey.

For the first time in my life, the sky arched blue and free all around me, and I was free, too. The jagged peak of the mountain rose behind me. Below me lay a forested valley. And in between, buried somewhere in the rumpled foothills and narrow, rocky paths where animals and humans made their tiny ways ...

I set off down the mountainside, following the scent of food.

WORLD BOOK DAY

SHARE A STORY

From breakfast to bedtime, there's always time to discover and share stories together. You can . . .

1 TAKE A TRIP to your LOCAL BOOKSHOP

Brimming with brilliant books and helpful booksellers to share awesome reading recommendations, you can also enjoy booky events with your favourite authors and illustrators.

FIND YOUR LOCAL BOOKSHOP: booksellers.org.uk/ bookshopsearch

2 JOIN your LOCAL LIBRARY

That wonderful place where the hugest selection of books you could ever want to read awaits – and you can borrow them for FREE! Plus expert advice and fantastic free family reading events.

FIND YOUR LOCAL LIBRARY: gov.uk/local-library -services/

3 CHECK OUT the WORLD BOOK DAY WEBSITE

Looking for reading tips, advice and inspiration? There is so much for you to discover at **worldbookday.com**, packed with fun activities, games, downloads, podcasts, videos, competitions and all the latest new books galore.

Illustrations © Rob Biddulph

SPONSORED BY

NATIONAL **BOOK** tokens

Celebrate stories. Love reading.